Little
HORRORS
The Spider Man

CHARD BOOKS

I couldn't believe my eyes.

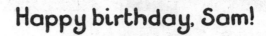

Mum had given me a birthday
card with a huge, hairy spider in it.

"That's not funny!" said Dad. "You know we don't like spiders."

"Especially big, fat, furry ones," said my sister, Kim.

7

Then Dad gave me a *nice* birthday surprise. He said we were going to the museum!

I couldn't wait to see the dinosaur bones.

Mum dropped us off at the station.

On the train we sat opposite an old lady.

Her dog was watching something…

A spider was dangling from the
luggage rack above a group of boys!

One of the boys pulled at the
spider's long hairy legs, and laughed.
Phew! It was just a joke spider.

When the boys got off the train, they rushed down the platform as though they were running away from something.

We decided to get a drink.
As we walked down the carriage,
Kim said, "Look, Sam!"

The spider was back.

It was dangling from a long piece of string. A strange-looking man was holding the other end.

His fingers were long and spindly
and his eyebrows were fat and hairy.
He was talking to two women.

In the buffet car, Dad joked, "Didn't that man look just like a spider?"

When we went back to our seats, the Spider Man was alone.
The women had disappeared!

"I bet he's wrapped them up in his spider's web!" whispered Dad.

But he hadn't really.
I spotted them leaving the train when we got to the next stop.

I picked up my comic to try to forget about spiders. It didn't work.

Then, the train went into a tunnel.

Suddenly, the brakes screeched,
and we slid to a halt.

The lights went out...

...and everything went quiet.

The guard's voice came over the crackly loudspeaker.

Don't worry!
Everything's under control!

Sitting in the dark, I felt something bristly touch my skin.

Was it a very hairy spider's leg?

Something cold and wet slid across my hand.

It made a strange, slurpy noise.

The spider was eating me!

Then the emergency lights flickered on, and in the eerie glow I saw...

...it was the old lady's dog.

My heart was still beating fast.
Out of the gloom, a figure lurched
towards us.

"Do you like my little friend?" it asked.

It was the Spider Man!

Before I could answer, an enormous
spider dropped from his hand.

I was glad it hadn't landed on me.

The Spider Man chuckled, and
pulled a jar out of his coat pocket.
Inside, was the hairiest, scariest
spider I had ever seen.

It wasn't a toy.
It was real!

I opened my mouth to scream,
but no sound came out.

Then the Spider Man opened the jar.
"This," he said, "is a Mexican
Jumping Spider!"

He shook the spider onto the table.
My skin turned cold and damp.

Very gently, he poked the spider.

It shot into the air!

And so did we!

The Spider Man caught it in the jar, and quickly put the lid back on.

He was very pleased with himself.

"Now," he said. "Let me introduce you to my very special friend, Boris."

I did *not* want to meet Boris. I
wanted to run away. But I couldn't
move. I felt as though I was trapped
in the Spider Man's web.

Slowly, from out of his top pocket, crawled a horrible, humungous, terrifying…TARANTULA!

The Spider Man softly stroked
Boris's back, and the spider smiled.

The web seemed to tighten around
me. I couldn't breathe.

Then the main lights came on. The train creaked, and began to move.

The Spider Man put Boris away.

"It's so nice to meet people who like spiders," he said. "They're such cuddly creatures, aren't they?"

He scuttled off to wait by the door.
At last, I could breathe again.

When we got to the museum, my heart stopped.

"So he really *is* a Spider Man!" gasped Kim.

I still wanted to see the dinosaur
bones, so Dad went to buy our tickets.
The Spider Man was talking to
some of his fans.

He didn't see us.

But Boris did.

He peeked out of the Spider Man's top pocket and…

…waved a long hairy leg!

Look out for these brilliant books from Orchard!

Little Horrors by Shoo Rayner

- ❏ The Swamp Man — 1 84121 646 1
- ❏ The Pumpkin Man — 1 84121 644 5
- ❏ The Spider Man — 1 84121 648 8
- ❏ The Sand Man — 1 84121 650 X

Finger Clicking Reads by Shoo Rayner

- ❏ Rock-a-doodle-do! — 1 84121 465 5
- ❏ Treacle, Treacle, Little Tart — 1 84121 469 8

Grandpa Turkey's Tall Tales by Jonathan Allen

- ❏ King of the Birds — 1 84121 877 4
- ❏ And Pigs Might Fly — 1 84121 710 7

The One and Only by Laurence Anholt and Tony Ross

- ❏ Micky the Muckiest Boy — 1 86039 983 5
- ❏ Ruby the Rudest Girl — 1 86039 623 2
- ❏ Harold the Hairiest Man — 1 86039 624 0

And many more!